Thomas de Celano, Franklin Johnson

The Dies Irae

an English version in double rhymes - with an essay and notes

Thomas de Celano, Franklin Johnson

The Dies Irae
an English version in double rhymes - with an essay and notes

ISBN/EAN: 9783337264222

Printed in Europe, USA, Canada, Australia, Japan

Cover: Foto ©Andreas Hilbeck / pixelio.de

More available books at **www.hansebooks.com**

The Dies Iræ.

PRIVATELY PRINTED.

Cambridge, Mass.

1883.

The Dies Iræ.

AN ENGLISH VERSION IN DOUBLE
RHYMES, WITH AN ESSAY
AND NOTES.

By FRANKLIN JOHNSON.

1883.

PREFACE.

In 1865 I published in a religious journal a translation of the Dies Iræ in double rhymes. When the glamour of composition had passed away, the defects of my performance were so apparent that I determined to correct them. I did not suppose that the task would prove arduous; but though so long a time has elapsed, my ideal is still far above my attainment. The work occupied my attention at frequent intervals for fifteen years, and I think that in few months of this period did I fail to make some progress. There were weeks in succession during which, both day and night, my mind was filled with the stanzas. At such seasons, the moment that I gained a little leisure, they

would appear before me like an army march-
ing with thundrous cadence. I could not
have dismissed them had I desired; but I
did not wish to do so. The verses, like the
names of flowers, have a charm even for
those who do not know their meaning. But
one familiar with the sense finds in them an
unexampled appeal to the heart, to the
imagination, to terror, to hope; and if he
engages in the tantalizing effort to set forth
in English their burden of thought, their
sublime pictures, frequently dashed in with
a single word, their throbs of emotion,
their weird measure, and their delicate asso-
nances, he falls under a fascination at once
awful and delightful. The occupation has
often assisted me to conquer care, and has
brought me refreshment.

No man has a better right than that of its
author to criticise a production; and I am
well aware how much my translation is lack-

ing in the life and movement of the original :

The marble shows the form and face ;
But who shall give it vital grace?

To the inherent difficulties of the task,
recognized by all who have attempted it, is
added now the necessity of avoiding ground
already occupied by others ; and this requires
great solicitude, so numerous are the versions,
and so various are the forms of ingenuity
exhibited in their structure.

CAMBRIDGE, MASS.,
    November 10, 1883.

THE DIFFICULTIES

Versions of the Dies Iræ in single rhymes may be made with great facility; and it is remarkable that those stanzas which are most difficult to render in double rhymes are the easiest to produce in the other form. Take the first, for example:

Day of wrath! Ah me, that day!
Earth in flame shall pass away:
Thus both Psalm and Sibyl say.

But the versions in single rhymes lack an essential element of the charm which the Latin possesses, and are chiefly interesting

because, though they fail to give the cadance
and the feeling of the original, they may be
made quite literal. I dismiss them, therefore,
and in the rest of this essay I shall speak
only of versions in double rhymes.

The chief requisite of a translation is that
it conform to the rules of its own language, while it exhibits the spirit, as well as
the sense of the original. This is expressed
well by Jowett in his second edition of Plato :
" It may seem a truism to assert that an English translation must have a distinct meaning,
and must be English. Its object is not
merely to render the words of one language
into the words of another, but to produce an
impression similar, or nearly similar, to that
of the original on the mind of the reader.
It should be rhythmical and varied, and,
above all, equable in style. It should in
some degree, at least, retain the characteristic
qualities of the ancient writer, his freedom,

grace, simplicity, stateliness, weight, precision ; or the best part of him will be lost to the English reader. It should read as an original work, and should also be the most faithful transcript which can be made of the language from which the translation is taken, consistently with the first requirement of all. that it be English." Specially in the translation of a poem should the feeling of the original. as well as the form, be preserved. It is small praise to say that it is literal, for it may be this. and still not rise above the dignity of prose.

But the difficulties which attend the translation of the Dies Iræ into English, while adhering to its proper form, are so great that he who undertakes the task is constantly tempted either to violate the laws of our language, or to sacrifice the spirit of the original in order to conform to the letter. The faults into which he is most liable to fall are the following :

I.   His sentences may be incomplete, if
not ungrammatical.   The version of the late
General John A. Dix is perhaps more nearly
literal than any other in double rhymes : but
it presents several instances of this defect.
I quote the first and the seventeenth stanzas
as examples :

Day of vengeance, lo ! that morning
On the earth in ashes dawning,
David with the Sibyl warning.

Low in supplication bending.
Heart as though with ashes blending.
Care for me when all is ending.

I may instance also the third stanza of
Périè :

Then shall trumpet. widely sounding.
From their graves, with noise astounding,
Call the dead, the throne surrounding.

II. Still another defect is that of constructions which, though not strictly incorrect, strike the reader as makeshifts. Dix, had he been writing a thought of his own in English verse, could not have cast it in this form :

Death and Nature, mazed, are quaking,
When, the grave's deep slumber breaking,
Man to judgment is awaking.

Nor could Périè have said :

Ah, what trembling, ah, what fearing,
When the upright Judge appearing,
Will from doubt be all things clearing.

Nor could Rev. William R. Williams, D. D., have expressed himself thus :

Ah that day ! that day of weeping !
When, in dust no longer sleeping,
Man to God in guilt is going : —
Lord, be, then, thy mercy showing.

The fault of the last line in each of these stanzas is evident.

III.   A not uncommon defect is the transference of some idiom peculiar to the Latin language.   The versions of Abraham Coles, M. D., are admirable for their vigor of expression, but they afford several instances in point:

Trumpet, scattering sounds of wonder,
Rending sepulchers asunder,
Shall resistless summons thunder.

Book, where actions are recorded,
All the ages have afforded,
Shall be brought and dooms awarded.

Had the writer been composing an English poem. it would not have occurred to him to omit the definite article when speaking of the trumpet and the book.   The exigencies of translation alone induced him so to strain the rules of English composition.

IV. Another fault is that of rhymes so imperfect as not to be allowable. Almost all the versions contain them. The first stanza of Dix has been cited already as an instance of defective grammar; but it is equally defective in rhyme:

Day of vengeance, lo! that morning
On the earth in ashes dawning,
David with the Sibyl warning.

The version of Williams is one of the best, and if I cite his ninth and seventeenth stanzas as instances under this head, it is not because I fail to appreciate his work as a whole:

Jesus, Lord, my plea let this be,
Mine the wo that brought from bliss Thee;
On that day, Lord, wilt Thou miss me?

Bowed and prostrate hear me crying;
Heart in dust before Thee lying:
Lord, my end, O be Thou nigh in.

V. The difficulty of finding double rhymes in English has led almost all the translators to make a very free use of the present participle. But the frequent repetition of rhymes formed in this manner wearies the ear. Indeed, I am convinced that two stanzas ending thus should never be permitted to come together. How hard it is to observe this rule may be learned by a glance at the versions. The first six stanzas of Dix have lines terminating uniformly in the present participle, as have the first three of Williams. In the admirable translation of W. J. Irons this fault has been wholly avoided, and it is less conspicuous in the translations of Coles than in many others.

VI. In their desire to preserve the double rhymes and the fascinating measure of the Latin hymn, the translators have been almost compelled to employ words unsuited to serious poetry, like "compensation" and "nugatory" in the following stanzas from Coles:

Awful Monarch of Creation!
Saving without compensation,
Save me, Fountain of Salvation!

Thou, the Lord of Life and Glory,
Hung'st a victim gashed and gory:
Let not all be nugatory.

VII. Another defect arises from the effort
to find in English an equivalent for every
phrase of the Latin, so that to this end rhyme
and accent are sacrificed. The false rhyme
of Dix in his first stanza, which I have already
cited, was tolerated in order to make a place
for the "David cum Sibylla" of the original.
The "Deus" of the last stanza has betrayed
many translators into faulty accent. Périè
halts thus:

Oh God, spare him, we implore Thee!

A defect still more serious may be classed
under the same head, since it is owing to the

same motive.   Not infrequently the chief thought of the stanza is obscured in order to preserve a semblance of some word or epithet which is not absolutely essential to the argument.   In the first two stanzas the author sketches in graphic lines the larger features of the scene, the burning world and the quaking multitudes, without regard to the succession of events.   In the following three, the order is observed, and the blast of the trumpet, the resurrection of the dead, the appearing of the book, and the enthronement of the Judge, are painted in awful colors.   The soul now finds itself in vision before the bar where even the righteous tremble, and casts about for some source of hope.   The approach of despair is checked, as the eyes fall on the King Himself, who is also the Savior ; and the next three stanzas plead His passion as a ground of mercy.   In the eleventh stanza the writer reflects that in fact he is still in the flesh, that

the perils in which in imagnation he had
placed himself have not yet appeared, and
that when they shall come it will be too late
for prayer; he therefore asks for pardon before the end of time, which is to be the end of
probation. In the twelfth, thirteenth, and
fourteenth stanzas, he confesses his sins, and ex-
presses his confidence in divine grace. In the
fifteenth and sixteenth his fancy recurs to the
terrors which had filled it in the beginning,
though not with the same degree of pain. In
the seventeenth stanza we have, apparently,
an instance of that curious facility with
which all believers associate death and the
Second Advent of Christ; the suppliant begs
for divine assistance in the closing hours of
life, as if these were to be the closing
hours of the whole earth, the period to
which he had looked forward with such
apprehension. In the last stanza he remem-
bers once more the human race risen from

the grave to receive the deeds done in the
body, and he beseeches God to spare the
guilty.

Such is the current of this passionate
prayer. But in our translations, the sub-
sidiary thoughts with which it is associated
may become so prominent as to hide the
stream that they were intended only to adorn.
The versions of the seventeenth stanza
present numerous instances. The feeling is
that of a soul contrite in view of sin ; and it
is represented by the bowed form and the
heart crushed as ashes. Poe says: "We
should so render the original that the version
should impress the people for whom it is
intended, just as the original impressed the
people for whom it was intended." No
other rule for the translator can be given.
And if he conforms to it he will be more
solicitous to express with adequate emotion
the penitence with which this stanza is bur-

dened, than to find some faint likeness of its mere verbiage. But in these lines of Coles, the thought is forgotten in order that language distantly resembling the Latin may be employed:

I beseech Thee, prostrate lying,
Heart as ashes, contrite, sighing,
Care for me when I am dying!

The "crushed heart" of the original has a definite meaning, which is only concealed by the "heart as ashes" of the version, a phrase that conveys no thought whatever. There is equally little signification in the rendering of Dix:

Heart as though with ashes blending.

Another example is the "humbly creeping' of Périè:

Suppliant and humbly creeping,
Heart with anguish wrung and weeping,
Have me in Thy holy keeping!

It would be idle for me to suppose that I had overcome all the difficulties which have proved so serious to others. This study of their labors admonishes me that many defects will be found in my own. Perhaps the Dies Iræ will not take a permanent place among English hymns till some one shall choose from the many translations the best stanzas of each, and shall weave his selections together. I venture to hope, as the utmost height of my anticipation. that when such a final version shall appear, a few of my lines may be found in it.

DIES IRÆ.

Dies iræ. dies illa!
Solvet sæclum in favilla.
Teste David cum Sibylla.

Quantus tremor est futurus.
Quando Judex est venturus.
Cuncta stricte discussurus!

Tuba mirum spargens sonum
Per sepulchra regionum.
Coget omnes ante thronum.

Mors stupebit. et Natura,
Quum resurget creatura
Judicanti responsura.

Liber scriptus proferetur.
In quo totum continetur.
Unde mundus judicetur.

Judex ergo quum sedebit.
Quidquid latet apparebit,
Nil inultum remanebit.

Quid sum miser tunc dicturus?
Quem patronum rogaturus,
Quum vix justus sit securus?

Rex tremendæ majestatis.
Qui salvandos salvas gratis,
Salva me, fons pietatis.

Recordare, Jesu pie.
Quod sum causa tuæ viæ:
Ne me perdas illa die.

Quærens me sedisti lassus;
Redemisti crucem passus;
Tantus labor non sit cassus.

Juste Judex ultionis,
Donum fac remissionis
Ante diem rationis.

Ingemisco tanquam reus:
Culpa rubet vultus meus:
Supplicanti parce, Deus.

Qui Mariam absolvisti,
Et latronem exaudisti,
Mihi quoque spem dedisti.

Preces meæ non sunt dignæ,
Sed tu bonus fac benigne,
Ne perenni cremer igne.

Inter oves locum præsta,
Et ab hædis me sequestra,
Statuens in parte dextra.

Confutatis maledictis,
Flammis acribus addictis,
Voca me cum benedictis.

Oro supplex et acclinis,
Cor contritum quasi cinis,
Gere curam mei finis.

Lachrymosa dies illa,
Qua resurget ex favilla
Judicandus homo reus;
Huic ergo parce, Deus!

DAY OF WRATH.

Day of wrath, that day of burning!
Earth shall end, to ashes turning:
Thus sing Saint and Seer discerning.
How
~~Then~~ shall quake both high and lowly
When the Judge shall come, most holy,
Strict to search all sin and folly!

Then is heard a sound of wonder!
Mighty blasts of trumpet-thunder
Rend the sepulchers asunder!

Death and Nature reel and tremble
As the rising throngs assemble:
What can ere that woe resemble!
my soul,
Vain, ~~how vain!~~ is all concealing;
For the book is brought, revealing
Every deed and thought and feeling.

Thereupon, the Judge is seated,
And our sins are loud repeated,
And to each is vengeance meted.

Wretched me! How gain a hearing,
Where the righteous falter, fearing,
At the pomp of His appearing?

King of majesty and splendor,
Fount of pity, true and tender,
Be, Thyself, my strong defender.

From Thy woes my hope I borrow:
I did cause Thy way of sorrow:
Do not lose me on that morrow.

Seeking me. Thou weary sankest.
Nor from scourge and cross Thou shrankest;
Make not vain the cup Thou drankest.

Thou wert righteous even in slaying;
Yet forgive my guilty straying,
Now, before that day dismaying.

Though my sins with shame suffuse me,
Though my very moans accuse me,
Canst Thou, Loving One, refuse me!

Blessed hope! I have aggrieved Thee:
Yet, by grace, the Thief believed Thee,
And the Magdalen received Thee.

Though unworthy my petition,
Grant me full and free remission,
And redeem me from perdition.

Be my lot in love decreed me:
From the goats in safety lead me:
With Thy sheep forever feed me.

When Thy foes are all confounded,
And with bitter flames surrounded,
Call me to Thy bliss unbounded.

From the dust, I pray Thee, hear me:
When my end shall come, be near me;
Let Thy grace sustain and cheer me.

Ah, that day, that day of weeping,
When, no more in ashes sleeping,
Man shall rise and stand before Thee!
Spare him, spare him, I implore Thee.

NOTES ON SOME OF THE STANZAS.

THE FIRST.

Several translators have sought to preserve in English the "favilla" and the "David cum Sibylla" of the original. But little success has attended these efforts, as they have required a too costly sacrifice of grace, of grammar and of rhyme. The following, from the first version of Coles, is perhaps the best that can be done with " favilla :"

Day of prophecy! It flashes,
Falling spheres together dashes.
And the world consumes to ashes.

In the first edition of his Dies Iræ, Dix presented a translation of this stanza which,

for its high finish, its delicate suggestion of
the antique, and its perfection of form,
has never been surpassed:

Day of vengeance, without morrow!
Earth shall end in flame and sorrow,
As from Saint and Seer we borrow.

His desire to make a place for " David cum
Sibylla " was one of the motives which
induced him to discard these elegant lines,
for this dreadful substitute:

Day of vengeance, lo! that morning
On the earth in ashes dawning,
David with the Sibyl warning.

After much study, I have been forced, in
common with the majority of the translators,
to content myself with a paraphrase.

The Sixth.

My sixth stanza is somewhat like that of
Williams, quoted below. The lines had
escaped my memory when my own were
written. I trust that the differences are suffi-
cient to warrant me in retaining my version.

Now the Sovran Judge is seated:
All, long hid, is loud repeated;
Naught escapes the judgment meted.

The Ninth.

In my translation I use the word "morrow" in its well-recognized sense of morning.
This stanza is one of the easiest to render
literally in single rhymes:

O remember, Lord, I pray,
It was I that caused Thy way:
Do not lose me on that day.

But no stanza resists more stubbornly the
effort to translate it in double rhymes. The
difficulty arises in part from the obscurity of
the language, which has no precise meaning
for the ordinary Protestant reader, and hence
needs at once to be interpreted and trans-
lated. It may be chiefly for this reason that
all the translators resort to paraphrase.
What was the " way" of Jesus, which the
penitent declares that he caused? Périè under-
stands His whole earthly career of humilia-
tion :

Bear in mind Thy pious mission
To redeem my lost condition :
Save me, Jesus, from perdition.

Thus also Coles in all his versions. Irons
looks rather at the Incarnation, the "way"
into the world :

Think, kind Jesu' — my salvation
Caused Thy wondrous Incarnation ;
Leave me not to reprobation.

Dix appears to have in view the last sad moments of our Lord's earthly career, though his language is not definite :

Jesus. think of Thy wayfaring,
For my sins the death-crown wearing ;
Save me. in that day. despairing.

To a Romanist the signification is clear. He has heard much of the "via dolorosa." through which our Savior bore His cross. A street in Jerusalem is still known by the name, and legend points it out as that along which He took His weary way to die for us. The stations in the church, where the Romanist pauses to pray. have pictures representing this journey. To the Romanist the "way" of Christ is a conception as definite as is His "cup" to the Protestant. I have no doubt that Thomas de Celano was thinking of the "via dolorosa" when he wrote the hymn. and that he considered it a symbol of all

the sufferings which the Son of God endured.
In my version I have sought to preserve this
thought, though at some sacrifice of the first
line.

But there is another source of obscurity.
What is the argument urged in the stanza?
It is not expressed fully. Perhaps it might
be presented in the forms of logic somewhat
as follows, though in my version I have cho-
sen to adhere more closely to the disjointed
structure of the original :

It was I that caused Thy sorrow,
Therefore save me on that morrow.

I will add that I have been inclined at
times to prefer the following. though it is a
paraphrase rather than a translation :

Mine the woe that hither drew Thee :
Mine the sin that pierced and slew Thee :
Mine be hope and mercy through Thee.

THE TENTH.

There are no finer lines in any version than the following, by Williams, equally excellent as a translation of the Latin, and as a stanza of an English hymn:

Wearily for me Thou soughtest:
On the cross my soul Thou boughtest;
Lose not all for which Thou wroughtest.

The first line of my version is identical with that of Coles: but as a whole mine is different from his, and, I think, more nearly literal. He renders the stanza thus:

Seeking me Thou weary sankest,
All my cup of trembling drankest,
Full of reddest wrath and rankest.

THE THIRTEENTH.

The following is almost literal. I should have inserted it in the text of my version, were it not for the word shrive, to which there are objections. First, it is a sectarian term, and is used in general with reference to the Romish Church : but the Dies Iræ is singularly free from everything peculiar to the communion of which its author was a member. Second, it means, according to the dictionaries, "to confess" a person, and thus covers a wider ground than that of mere forgiveness, though it includes this. In our later Protestant literature it is employed frequently as a synonym of "pardon," "absolve," where the confessional is mentioned; but since the lexicographers do not recognize the validity of this restricted use. I cannot follow it without misgiving. Though the stanza must be condemned on these grounds. I think it sufficiently accurate as a translation, and sufficiently rhythmical, to merit a place in these notes :

He by whom the Thief was shriven
And the Magdalen forgiven
Grants to me the hope of Heaven.

THE SEVENTEENTH.

Does "mei finis" refer to death, or to the last day, as the end of the trial which the suppliant, in common with all men, is undergoing? The difficulty of preserving in English the exact words "my end," has led the larger number of translators to resort to paraphrase, in which they attempt to interpret the meaning, some taking one side of the question which I have asked, and some the other. I have preferred to make a close translation, that the English reader may form his own judgment. I might treat the expression as

referring to death, however, with equal facility, as in the following lines :

In the dust behold me lying,
While my broken heart is sighing
For Thy love when I am dying.

If anyone prefers the other view, it may be
presented in this manner :

In the dust behold me bending ;
Hear my sighs to Thee ascending ;
Comfort me when all is ending.